The I'M NOT SCARED Book

To Liza. Love, Todd

The I'M NOT SCARED Book

Todd Parr

SCHOLASTIC INC.

Sometimes I'm scared of the dark.

I'm not scared if I have a night-light.

Sometimes I'm scared of dogs.

I'm not scared when they give me kisses.

Sometimes I'm scared to ride
on an airplane.

Sometimes I'm scared of monsters and ghosts.

I'm not scared when I see that they aren't real.

Sometimes I'm scared of what's under my bed.

I'm not scared once I clean everything out and see all my favorite toys.

Sometimes I'm scared when my family argues.

I'm not scared when we hug and say I'm sorry.

I'm not scared when I wear them
on my head.

I'm not scared when I stay close to Mommy.

Sometimes I'm scared on my first day of school.

Sometimes I'm scared of thunder and lightning.

I'm not scared when I build a fort
with my best friend.

Sometimes I'm scared when
I do something wrong.

I'm not scared when I help to fix it.

Sometimes I'm scared I will make a mistake.

I'm not scared when I know
I tried my best.

Sometimes I'm scared I'm not perfect.

I'm not scared when I meet someone just like me.

Sometimes we are scared of things 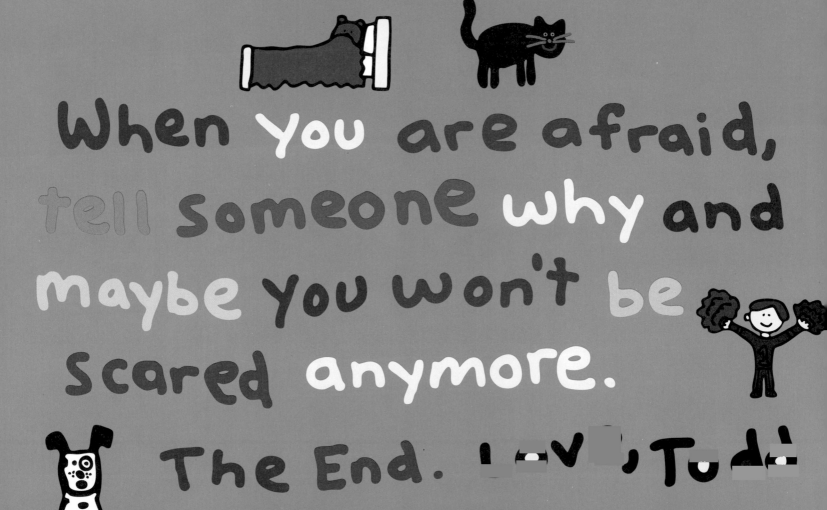 because we don't understand them.

When you are afraid, tell someone why and maybe you won't be scared anymore.

The End. Love, Todd

Todd Parr is the author of more than thirty books for children, including the *New York Times* bestselling *The I Love You Book*. He lives in Berkeley, California.

Also by Todd Parr:

The I Love You Book

It's Okay to Be Different

The Earth Book

The Peace Book

We Belong Together

The Mommy Book

The Daddy Book

The Grandma Book

The Grandpa Book

The Family Book

Reading Makes You Feel Good

The Feelings Book

The Feel Good Book

For a complete list of
Todd's books and more information, please visit
www.toddparr.com

ISBN 978-0-545-91793-3

Copyright © 2011 by Todd Parr. All rights reserved.
Published by Scholastic Inc., 557 Broadway, New York, NY 10012,
by arrangement with Little, Brown Books for Young Readers,
a division of Hachette Book Group, Inc. SCHOLASTIC and associated logos are
trademarks and/or registered trademarks of Scholastic Inc.

12 11 10 9 8 7 6 5 4 3 2 1   15 16 17 18 19 20/0

Printed in the U.S.A.   40

First Scholastic printing, October 2015